A Little Book of All Kinds

Reshma Cheknath Umesh

Ukiyoto Publishing

All global publishing rights are held by

Ukiyoto Publishing

Published in 2022

Content Copyright © Reshma C 2022

ISBN 9789360165673

*All rights reserved.
No part of this publication may be reproduced,
transmitted, or stored in a retrieval system, in any
form by any means, electronic, mechanical,
photocopying, recording or otherwise, without the
prior permission of the publisher.*

The moral rights of the author have been asserted.

*This is a work of fiction. Names, characters,
businesses, places, events, locales, and incidents are
either the products of the author's imagination or
used in a fictitious manner. Any resemblance to
actual persons, living or dead, or actual events is
purely coincidental.*

*This book is sold subject to the condition that it shall
not by way of trade or otherwise, be lent, resold,
hired out or otherwise circulated, without the
publisher's prior consent, in any form of binding or
cover other than that in which it is published.*

To all children and grown-up children

Acknowledgement

Umesh P Menon (My husband) – Great gratitude for your support and understanding.

&

Thank you, Martini (My dear doggy), for your endless love.

Illustrations inside the book
by Umesh P Menon

Contents

Preface

Fragments from a Diary	1
"Unawareness of our natural surroundings is a disgrace", sings a Blue Tit.	3
A Memory	6
Peach Curls	9
Who Am I?	13
Script Written for a Cookery Show	16
Sepia Effect	18
Confusion at an Afternoon Art Class	20
Poodle and a Sloth	24
About the Author	29

PREFACE

Our Earth is full of different kinds of species. Just like us humans, they all are full of life and are impossible to ignore. The more we learn about them the more we love and admire those species. Like, the moment I started loving and caring my dog, I realized the nature of their love, their life; happiness, routine, discipline, ability to be in the present, strength, and their nature to settle down to few things without greed. These characteristics allured me more towards the other animals and their life.

If you keep observing an animal, you will realize how satisfied they are. Animals play a key role in protecting our environment.

With a sense of shame, I realize that I wasted much time and fun by not noticing the denizens of all kinds.

— Reshma Cheknath Umesh

Fragments from a Diary

Feb-7-1999

A fine day! I went for my usual evening walk. Plains were sinking into stillness. Such dusk falls often fill my mind with sudden fits of gloom and faint promises of pleasure, concurrently. Plain and dark tone of the air quickly filled with sounds of sea waves from the sky! Yes, the sound was directed from the western sky, where the night fall was slowly extinguishing its glow. I looked up at the distant murmur of the waves. What was that? An air show? No…No an apparition of a slowly moving giant bird?

It took few seconds for my ears and eyes to synchronize with the magical mystery of Nature's majestic murmuration and synchronization. It was an aerial show conducted by the super stars of the sky – Starlings. They were hundreds or, may be, thousands in number flying in perfect harmony. So fine were their moves that their circles and waves recalled ebb and flow of the sea. Forming circles of various forms and shapes they conducted a wondrous aerial display. They took me to a state of reverie with their lively musical whistles and I prayed and thanked Almighty for this blessing. I felt myself to be so lucky to be able to witness this wonderful phenomenon. Such moments are to be cherished as it rarely comes in a lifetime. A sigh of relief escaped me, and I said to myself while returning home, "Starlings appeared and disappeared out of nowhere, so swift, so brief but everlasting."

Above written fragments were taken from my brother's diary who was a traveller. Starlings always used to fascinate me and my brother due to their peculiarities. These amazing birds are also known as super stars of the ground, as their skills are not just restricted to the sky. They reassert their supremacy both up and down. They are superheroes. Care to know?

They have this astonishing skill of mimicking sounds. These keen observers can mimic various kinds of sounds like the other aerial species, telephone bell, train sounds, car alarm, human calls etc. They even have the history of duplicating a referee's whistle and cancelling a football match.

Starlings are beauty with brains. These intelligent birds also take good feather care by anting, oiling and bathing in water.

Here I am taking my leave. Wishing you all 'Starling luck', that may the stunning Starlings greet your eyes. Because, Starlings are stunning, indeed!

"Unawareness of our natural surroundings is a disgrace", sings a Blue Tit.

How less cognizant we all are to our natural surroundings!

How less awareness we have of our environment!

How little appreciation we provide to other species that surrounds us!

How much I am impressed but how little I can express;

Out of shame of a camouflage,

Of a wide and brilliant eyespot.

How much I am impressed but how little I can express!

No mention was made, how silly superficial predator I made!

No mention I make of my prey's swift veil,

For all my historical ventures are now in vain.

For how much I am ashamed and how little I can explain,

a shameful escape of a nitwit Blue Tit.

A prose poetry.

Written by,

A Blue Tit bird.

Poetry Analysis:

This poetry is written by a Blue Tit bird. Tone of the poetry is – 'Sadness.'

Prey mentioned above is a Peacock butterfly.

Metre used by the poet here is iambirdiebluetit metre. Many words in these lines of poetry have stressed syllables due to heavy stress.

Theme of the poetry – To find out the theme let us break down Blue Tit's poetry.

Blue Tit begins the poetry by talking about awareness we all need to be having of our natural surroundings. Having meagre knowledge of Nature will lead us to disgrace. The recurring message poet uses here is the silliness he felt as a predator in front of his own prey, Peacock butterfly. Poet, as we can understand here, was venturing for his food and smelled his prey. But poet was unaware of his prey's eyespot's camouflaging techniques and caught off guard and thinks that he looked at the eyes of a larger animal and fled.

At first, let us understand more about our smarty here and then develop the idea into the main theme of the poem.

Peacock butterfly's eyespots are used to deter their predators. These majestic butterflies sits quietly with folded wings. Whenever a predator (here our poor poet) approaches this butterfly swiftly opens its wings revealing its eyespots. This swift camouflage confuses and scares the predator, which thinks that they are looking at the eyes of a monster animal. We cannot blame our poor Blue Tit here as the magically attractive bright colour of these wonderful flies can lure anyone.

This loss or rather lack of awareness which was capable to put a scar on his hunting career (which never happened before) is what the poet laments here. However, the poet ends his poetry with a positive note of hope. He concludes the poem wishing that may this new awareness lead us all to notice the wonders of our beautiful Nature in a fresh way.

A Memory

I always cherish memories, especially those sweet ones from the childhood. I wish to share one of my childhood days here. Call it a nostalgia, times of past, times I have passed or whatever. But for me, it is the joy of innocence. Here I share…

My dear mother always wakes me up with softness. Either by a soft kiss or by a happy news. That sweet morning, she said gently,

"Get up! Rise and shine Johnny. Today we have some special guests whose name can you guess? Though timid, they proved their love for us by coming back to our farm for 8 years."

With full excitement I jumped out of bed rubbing my eyes and asked mother,

"Who are they?"

To which mom replied,

"They sing exotic songs, dance and merry make. Exactly like their call they are very huge and fascinating to look at. Both male and female dance and sing duets."

Seeing my confused face mom added,

"I will sing a song which will help you to recollect your special guests."

And she sang,

"I bring spring with me or spring brings me with her! I don't know, don't know I, sings me the Crane."

"Oh my goodness! Dancing Cranes! Have they come? They are my favourite. I can't wait to see them. Now I know my Kungfu Crane", I said jumping up and down like a Crane in joy.

Mother took me to our backyard where the Cranes were happily singing. Without disturbing them we enjoyed listening to their loud songs and I asked Mom more about them.

She said, "Sandhill Cranes are very talkative with their family and care for their family's safety. Their race are, a kind of, successful birds in terms of how long they have been around on this Planet. Good that we humans have at least left them free from extinction. When are we going to completely understand the words like, 'co-existing and preserve' though we keep using it. Like Albert Einstein said,

"Any fool can know. The point is to understand."

Though successful, Cranes still face the threat of loss of wetland habitat. Just imagine a dry world without the colourful birds!

"How boring and ugly it will be!", I told mom.

"Cranes symbolizes teamwork, togetherness, hope, longevity and focus. Another interesting fact is, they sleep at night standing up on one leg. Now you sit here and enjoy watching the birds. Let me prepare breakfast for you."

Watching her opening the kitchen door, I called out,

"Mom, I want peanut butter jelly."

I still remember the smiling face of my mom. Her face was brightened up by the rays of the morning sun and in the background, the Cranes were singing love songs magically. Ahh! Those simple joys of childhood still add fuel to my life whenever it runs out of energy.

Peach Curls

Once upon a time there lived two happily married couples, Sandra and Sunny. Sunny and Sandra loved each other a ton. Their house was surrounded by the richness of green. It was a two-storeyed building with a huge garden. From the entrance of their house, Sunny planted many Peach trees which was his wife's favourite fruit tree. Couple cherished their happy moments in their garden.

One day Sandra decided to surprise her husband by colouring and curling her long and wavy hair. Without his knowledge she left home to a nearby ladies salon named, 'Manufacturing Beauties.' After indulging in a serious discussion with the hairdresser, she finally gave her consent to touch her hair. Thereafter, the confident hairdresser engaged herself very proudly in her nimble-fingered hair work.

Moments passed. Here comes out our Sandra with a peach-coloured curly hair. She was indeed a beauty to behold with her newly made peach curls.

Sandra was feeling quite happy about her new hair style. This happiness was visible as a blush on her lovely cheeks. Feeling very excited to surprise her husband she rushed home. But to her dismay, Sunny did not pay much attention to her hair. He was very busy in the garden.

'How can he do this to me? How could he ignore my peach curls? We both love peaches that's why I gave this colour to my hair. This is not fair! I was not expecting this reaction!'

Too many soliloquies troubled her mind. She talked her out of thinking by saying, "Sunny, I wish to drink peach juice for dinner. Let's pluck some."

To which Sunny replied coolly, "No peaches for dinner."

In a tone of surprise asked Sandra, "Why dear? You know I drink peach juice to stimulate the immune system and for my weight loss."

Sunny without looking at her side said plainly, "Peach curls! No peaches."

"Have your dinner and go to sleep dear. I am going out to meet a friend. Do not wait for me. I will be late," he added.

This neglect was unbearable for Sandra, and it wet her eyes.

"He didn't like my hair. He hates it. He didn't even utter a word about my peach curls. He has never said 'no' to me before. Today for the first time he said 'no' when I asked for some peach juice. All these happened because of these peach curls," she said weeping.

"I don't need you. I am going to change my hair colour back to black," saying this she rummaged through her wardrobe for a pack of black dye which she had bought before.

Moments passed. Here she stands in the balcony waiting eagerly for Sunny to be back home, playing with her black curls.

Sunny was back home carrying a brown bag printed, 'Ladies Apparels'.

It took some time for him to understand the mystery behind his wife's continual hair colour change. Paying attention to his wife's laments patiently he told her, "Oh, my poor Sandra! Do you know dear how much I fell in love with your hair makeover? I was so happy and I went out to buy you a gown which you once desired, to surprise you back. Why did you change your hair colour, my little impatient wifey?"

Seeing his wife's pain he added, "do not worry, black colour suits more for your natural beauty."

Quite astonished Sandra asked, "Then why did you say peach curls? No peaches! That plain rudeness of yours made me think so."

Bursting out laughter Sunny said, "You silly! I was talking about peach leaf curls. I thought you knew."

"Peach leaf curls!", exclaimed Sandra.

"Yes, infection that ruins leaves. Have you not noticed yet? It is easily identifiable because of its red colour and twisted shape. I never thought you could be unaware about your favourite peach fruit tree's wellbeing."

"Is that why you said no juice?", asked Sandra in a repenting tone.

"Yes. As they are ill they cannot produce much fruits. But still poor trees are trying their best to give us fruits. Though we neglect them they cannot bear to see our unhappy face."

These words wet Sandra's eyes and she lifted her window curtains to wish her favourite peach trees goodnight.

Who Am I?

Oo-de-lally, Oo-de-lally, golly, what a day!

Hey buddy, as you are here, let us play a game. What say? Okayyy?? So, let us play who am I?

- I am needed for balancing wetland ecosystem.

- I am an excellent swimmer and my eyes, ears & nose adapts well for swimming underwater. I can even stay underwater for many minutes. Can chew underwater and can swim backward too. Hmmm, too smart! I should pat my own back.

- I am quite famous for my plant-based house.

- I can build a house out of vegetation on still water with an underwater entrance door. I even have an earthen lodge adjacent to water; where my kits, I mean my tender children and family, resorts for winter. View from my waterfront lodge…what should I say – Buena vista!

- Coming back to the game…. I will give you another information about me. I am almost nocturnal and as per a myth my race dived to the bottom of primordial sea to bring the mud out of which Earth was created and I can even predict weather.

- I dine on a table made out of plants and mud.

- Now a bit about my ethical side… I lend my house to other species for rest and nest. I can be very co-operative, or you can say, I am quite willing to face challenges. But, if darn someone disrespects me and my family, I can be very aggressive.

Hey mate! I gave you enough clues and you know its quite difficult to self-praise. Now tell me who am I?

Are you willing to give up? Hmmm…

** Oo-de-lally, Oo-de-lally, golly, what a day!

(Song by Roger Miller)

Muskrat's Home

Script Written for a Cookery Show

Hello friends, welcome to my cookery show. Hope you all are safe and sound.

It is a beautiful day outside. Weather is very pleasant. Sun as always is burning itself to give us all life. Majestic rays from the Sun is adding extra beauty to all the ordinary making it look, extraordinary.

Hmm, as we have time constraints here let us start to cook. Today, I will share with you a recipe to become a good human being, 'Recipe for Being a Human.' Friends, it is very simple recipe. We only need few ingredients here.

First, take a big vessel and pour your infinite love for all kinds of plants. For sweetness, add your essence of love for the flowers. Give it sometime to blend.

Meanwhile, take infinite amount of your warm promises for nurturing and cultivating trees and blend it well with your oath to remain forever faithful to the Planet Earth. Pour this mixture into the vessel and stir it well.

Now it is time to season it with an unavoidable ingredient - your tenderness and care for all the animals. This is the spine of our recipe which will serve to fulfill the basic purpose of a human being on this Planet – to be a *responsible caretaker* of all the species, to live and let live.

Hey friends! I am getting a nice and sweet aroma here. Now it is time to serve this 'sweet human being' to our loving Mother Nature as a return gift; a giving back for everything we all accept each and every minute from Her. Hope you all enjoyed today's, 'Recipe for Being a Human.' Share your valuable feedback of living a life peacefully by 'Being a Human.' See you all soon. Bye.

Sepia Effect

A famous artist was once asked by an interviewer – "Who is your role model or rather who is your favourite painter, and which work by them allured you the most?"

Artist from the treasures of his heart brought forth a name. With a bit of struggle he said, "It is a bit difficult for me to answer. It remains as a secret in my mind's depth. This artist was resting in my mind's secret chamber, and I continued to dismiss this question for all these years. But today I think it is time for me to reveal my favourite natural painter."

"Tell us who is that person? I am quite sure your fan followers are eager to know," implored the impatient interviewer.

To which our renowned artist replied, "Sepia, my dear cuttlefish."

"A fish! It sounds quite fishy," added the puzzled interviewer in a funny way.

Completely ignoring the interviewer's comic effort the artist continued, "Yes! A great artist of all times. A gifted master painter who is the most intelligent of all invertebrates. I have spent many days and nights, quite fascinated, studying the great effort and focus of an artist, in a cuttle fish.

Like the other cephalopods; I mean squid, octopus etc, cuttle fish have very sophisticated eyes. It is simply wonderful to view her spectating her surroundings attentively and using her own body to re-create the beauty that she sees around. While the human artists have to depend on easels, paints, brushes, paper rolls and erasing tools our Sepia uses her own body to camouflage - to capture the art of her environment. Her aesthetic artistic talent never goes wrong. Indeed, a skillful master body artist I have ever known. She carries ink with her, though to spring away from the evil."

Interrupting the artist, the interviewer says in curiosity, "Now that explains the much-discussed Sepia effect of your work, I believe!"

"There you are. I hope it doesn't sound fishy for you now," added the artist.

And they both chuckled.

Confusion at an Afternoon Art Class

Scene - Confusion at an afternoon art class.

Characters - Madam Rebecca & Students (Catherine, Rose, Lavender, Elle, Pinky)

A small classroom with huge windows, few chairs and a broad table. Afternoon Sun rays have well-lighted the classroom. A huge Oak's branch was finding its way inside through the windows. A small chubby Robin was peacefully alighted on one of its branches. Heated murmuring of the students was gradually gaining prominence.

Catherine: I don't understand these confusions you all have caused. I am very much sure that Madam Rebecca told us to paint 'Bluebottles In a Cornfield.' So, it is definitely a flower not a fish!

Rose: I agree on that. It is not a fish as our dear Pinky says. But it could be a fly as well.

Elle: Yes, it is a fly but a butterfly. (pointing at her painting) by Bluebottle, Madam Rebecca meant a butterfly not any other flies.

Lavender: No! no, no (directing everybody's glance at her painting) I hope you all remember how strict Madam is, especially when it comes to painting. She was definitely asking us to paint Bluebottle Cornflower in a Cornfield.

Their heated conversations and confusions caused a disturbance to the Robin's afternoon nap, and it flew off to a nearby tree.

(Enters Madam Rebecca)

Madam Rebecca: Good Afternoon class! I hope you all are ready with your works. It is time for you to submit your paintings. One of you collect all the works and submit here.

Pinky took the charge of collection and kept it carefully one by one next to Madam. She kept her painting last in the row, as her friend's doubts have drained out her confidence completely. Madam was closely contemplating through the paintings. Tension amounting amongst the girls were clearly evident in the air.

Whose painting is going to win? Who is going to be right? What did she mean by Bluebottle? A fly? A butterfly? A flower? Or a fish? No! no it could never be a fish for sure!

Meanwhile, Madam Rebecca finally lay hold of Pinky's painting and a loud burst of laughter escaped her, very much unlike her.

Regaining her normal composure she said, Hmm, I went through all of your paintings. I think it is my mistake. I should have been clearer and more specific while giving you a topic. I could have explained a bit more. I wanted you all to paint a picture of Bluebottle flower, commonly known as cornflower or bachelor's button in a cornfield. I didn't think of Bluebottle fly and butterfly. But it is fine. You all did a wonderful job. All paintings are picturesque except (looked at Pinky with laughing eyes). Pinky, if you don't mind will you please explain the role of a Bluebottle fish in a cornfield? (looking quite amused she continued) Tell me what were you thinking dear or were you not even a bit thinking?

(Bell rings)

Madam: Ok! Will meet you all tomorrow and we will discuss more about your works. Good day everyone.

(leaves)

Everybody, visibly relieved, shifts their focus entirely to Pinky's painting and continued to tease her.

To which Pinky replies: You all are saved today only because of me. You should pat my back.

Catherine: Why?

Pinky: Have you ever seen her laughing before? At least I made her do that. My misplaced Portuguese man-of-war changed her mood and saved you all today. Thank me later. (exits)

(curtain falls)

Poodle and a Sloth

In the grey hours of a summer morning,
Somewhere on the Planet Earth
A poodle named Martini retired to rest.
Feeling so bored and dejected,
his usual gaymanner was disrupted by this
new lackadaisical temperament,
to which he decided to put an end to.
With a gentle seriousness he murmured,
"Let me go for a drive where the wild fields are awaiting my presence."
Losing no time, powdering, and perfuming himself
he set upon a long ride.
Sun rays were falling on his wonderful visage
as a sure sign of predilection.
Wind was lulling his ears while playing
with his golden fur.
Singing a song to himself he kept on driving at a
slow pace,

Until his eyes met a slow-moving sloth

lurking on his way.

Pausing his car with a sudden brake

here goes our warrior out

willing enough to relieve the tiny victim
from its chaos.

Here lies a brown-throated baby sloth

trying to cross the road.

"Oh! poor thing. You seem to be in misery," cried
Martini.

Perplexed and giving a troubled look baby sloth says,

"Me and my mother lives on the trees,

hanging upside down.

In a wildfire caused by the cigarettes, says mama,

we lost our tree house and mama went

in search of a new home and never returned.

I want to see my mama.

Take me to my mama, please," begs the poor one.

These words pierced through our super-sensitive
poodle.

Awakening to the sense of his moral responsibilities,

he took the beige coloured fugitive in hands.

Entitling himself to this little one's custody,

he walked in search of a habitat,

with a tail that wagged a thousand times.

It was a strange sight to behold!

To our valiant's astonishment he did not find

a thicket or a dell nearby.

But with a single-hearted determination he continued his venture, undistracted,

but had to end up by witnessing the bitter truth.

Unfortunately, it was only grey buildings and empty roads to be seen everywhere.

There was not any sign of green!

With a tiresome look in his eyes, he asked loudly,

"Where have all the trees gone?"

Losing all hope in humanity and sadly musing

over the agonies of animals and plants,

they both lapsed into silence.

A MODEST PROPOSAL

Let us love and be kind to all the animals as they are very wonderful to be with.

Also, from Reshma Cheknath Umesh, published by Ukiyoto

Dear Reader by Julie and Other Stories

About the Author

Reshma Cheknath Umesh

Reshma Cheknath Umesh is a Masters and Bachelors in English Language & Literature. She has worked as a College Professor in English Department. She is a published Author of the book 'Dear Reader by Julie and Other Stories'

Authors Official Instagram: *@reshmacheknathumesh*

.

www.ingramcontent.com/pod-product-compliance
Lightning Source LLC
LaVergne TN
LVHW041600070526
838199LV00046B/2061